But then a tic caused his head to shake,
followed by a noise he didn't mean to make.
Timid sadly looked at his friends' faces,
but funny stares, they had no traces.

Emma, age 6

"It's ok Timid," the two friends agreed,
"We are here for you, to help how you need.
Now that we talked about what is wrong,
we can understand and guide others along.
We will tell them it is just something you do.
Show them it is part of being you."

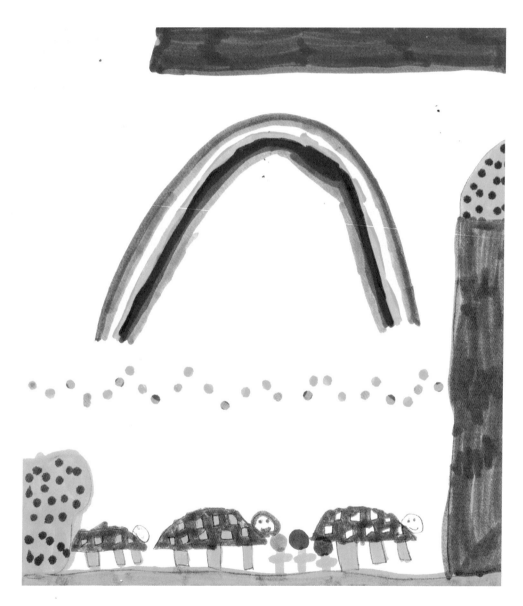

Brinnley, age 7

So Timid came all the way out,
and his friends gave a happy shout.
"Come play!" they called to Timid, and waved.
Having these friends made Timid brave.

Ryder, age 6

All three of them played the rest of the day
And about those tics --
no one noticed them anyway.

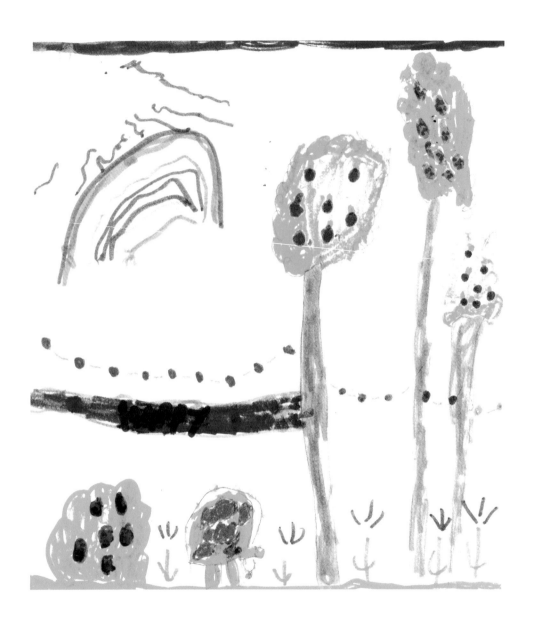

Lia, age 6

Aaron, age 7

# The Kindness Project

The Kindness Project began when Sandra witnessed a small act of kindness make a big difference to someone. At first it was just the book Kindness Kangaroo but then, with Brenda's help, ideas emerged for Empathy Elephant, Hopeful Hippo and Bravo Bear. Before they knew it, a whole alphabet of emotional animals arose.

Sandra and Brenda thought it was important to get ideas from children as to what they felt the emotion meant. When Sandra was asked into a classroom to discuss kindness, a new idea was created.

A different class participates in each book. Sandra visits the classroom and discusses the emotion with the children to gather ideas for the book. The story is then written to include some of their ideas. The completed story is sent to the class so that the children can each offer a drawing to help illustrate the book.

Sandra has been busy visiting schools all over Southern Ontario to read Kindness Kangaroo and get ideas for other books in the series. Soon, the entire alphabet series of books will be completed!

# About the Author

Sandra Wilson is a writer, educator and photographer looking to bring positivity, inspiration and fun into this world. She has a Bachelor of Arts in English and History and over 35 years of working with children. Sandra's stories are relatable, and they help children understand their struggles a little bit more. She loves to include the children in her stories and therefore most of her books involve a young illustrator. Please visit Sandra at www.quiteacharacter.ca.

Shajn, age 6

# Thank you to our sponsors!

## Kacy and Ange,
## Avery, Declan, and Rhys Johnson

## John, Lorraine
## and Jaclyn Wubben

## Rowan Reid and Kai Bailey

## Matt and Alicia,
## Ellena, Kade, and Hendrik Wubben

## Rob and Lynda Johnson

ONE THOUSAND TREES

HEWITT
JANCSAR
RESIDENTIAL & FARM REAL ESTATE

# Spotlight on Our Cover Illustrator
# 6-year-old Declan

My name is Declan and I am in Grade 2 but I drew the cover when I was in Grade 1. I have an older sister named Avery and a younger brother named Rhys. I love sports! This summer I was the pitcher for my softball team and I'm excited to give hockey a try this year. I was glad that Sandra came to my class to tell my friends that having tics is okay and that it is just a part of who I am.

## Thanks to our partner!

Cheyenne, age 6

Brady, age 7

Kai, age 6

# Be part of the Kindness Kangaroo Project

You can be part of the Kindness Kangaroo Project by purchasing a book, sponsoring the project or donating to help print the next book. For more information or to be a sponsor please visit www.quiteacharacter.ca.

For more information or to be a sponsor please visit www.quiteacharacter.ca.

"It's good that Sandra comes into the school to talk about emotions because kids get to talk about how they feel. Sometimes we don't know why we feel things."

Kayden, age 7

"The kids were so excited to see that you incorporated their ideas. As I was reading it to them they would be shouting out "Hey, that was what I said.""

Kristine, grade 1 teacher

# Timid Turtle

by Sandra Wilson

# Timid Turtle

Timid Turtle
ISBN: 978-1-988215-38-9

editing, layout and design by
*Saplings*
a branch of One Thousand Trees
www.onethousandtrees.com

in partnership with
Roots & Wings
*mental health awareness and empowerment through creativity*
www.ottrootsandwings.com

Printed in Toronto, Ontario, Canada by
Webcom Inc.

Timid Turtle
Written by Sandra Wilson
with ideas and illustrations from
the Grade 1 class of Mrs. Hodgins
Innerkip Central School
2017-2018

Keyan, age 6

Thank you to Christine and Brenda for your continued support.
Thanks to Declan, age 6, for drawing the cover!

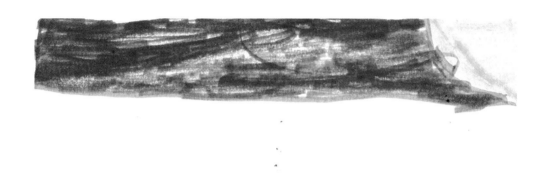

Lily, age 7

Timid Turtle was hiding in his shell
"What's the matter?" asked his friend.
"Are you not well?"
"I'm fine," Timid said. "That is, I'm not sick.
I'm just having trouble controlling my tic."
"What's a tic?" wondered his friend.
"Will it go away?"
"It is something I can't control," Timid
cried, "and it happens every day."

Cohen, age 7

"It is like a hiccup or a burp.
Sometimes my body gives
an uncontrolled jerk.
I can't stop it, it just happens to me.
So I don't want to come out
where others can see."

Noelle, age 7

"I'm sorry to hear that," his friend replied.
"But it's ok, you don't have to hide.
We are friends, which means
you shouldn't be scared.
The experiences we have are
something to be shared."

Ava, age 7

"I have glasses as you can see,
because my eyes don't work well for me.
So I look different with these on my face,
but they help me get from place to place.
At first I was afraid people
would call me names,
but then I realized I am still the same."

Hannah, age 7

Another friend came over just then,
because she wanted to play with them.
But Timid still hid away from stares.
He did not want to get laughs or glares.
He was so sad now he wanted to cry,
but both his friends encouraged him to try

Kyra, age 6

"I was scared to come to school today,
because my clothes don't fit the right way.
I have grown a lot and my clothes are tight.
When your clothes are too small
it can be a funny sight.
But I have friends that understand,
and will help me through it,
even hold my hand.
They helped me come out today,
and I want to help you the same way."

Alyssa, age 6

"Take a couple of deep breaths to start.
This will calm you and slow your heart.
Now let's talk about what you want to play,
something you can look forward to today."

Marco, age 6

The friends talked about all they could do,
and Timid found that his courage grew.
He poked his head out of his shell,
and saw smiles from his friends
telling him all was well.

Larson, age 7